THERE WAS AN OLD LADY WHO SWALLOWED A WORM!

by Lucille Colandro
Illustrated by Jared Lee

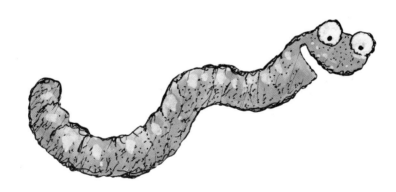

Cartwheel Books

an imprint of Scholastic Inc.
New York

For Evelyn and Leonardo and for our Earth, our home.
– L.C.

To PJ, You'll always be my lifetime sweetheart.
– J.L.

Text copyright © 2024 by Lucille Colandro.
Illustrations copyright © 2024 by Jared D. Lee Studios.

Library of Congress Cataloging-in-Publication Data available
ISBN 978-1-338-87913-1
10 9 8 7 6 5 4 3 2 1   24 25 26 27 28
Printed in the U.S.A.   40
First edition, February 2024

There was an old lady who swallowed a worm.
I don't know why she swallowed the worm,
but she started to squirm!

There was an old lady who swallowed some dirt.
It was just like dessert when she swallowed the dirt.

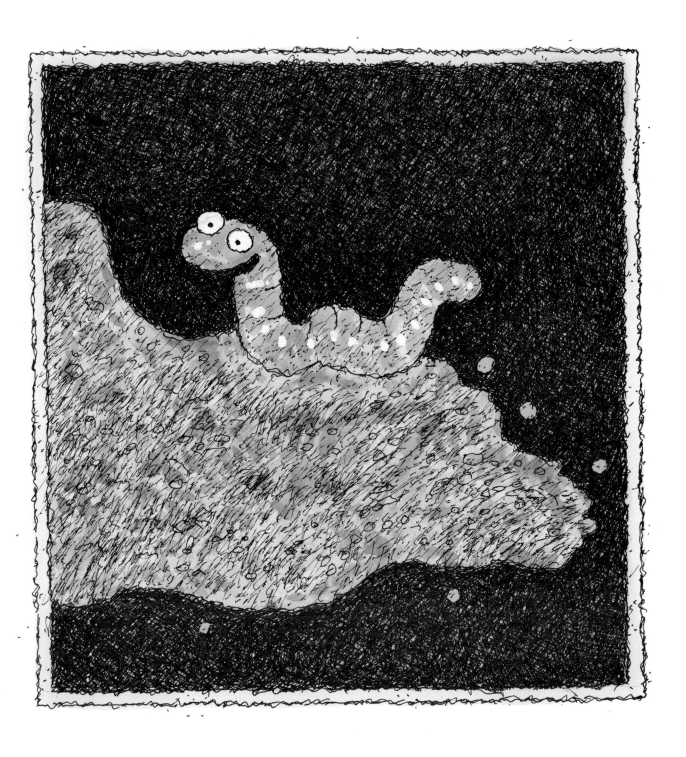

She swallowed the dirt so the worm could wiggle.
I don't know why she swallowed the worm,
but she started to squirm!

There was an old lady who swallowed a flower.
It was not sour, that pretty pink flower.

She swallowed the flower to plant in the dirt.
She swallowed the dirt so the worm could wiggle.

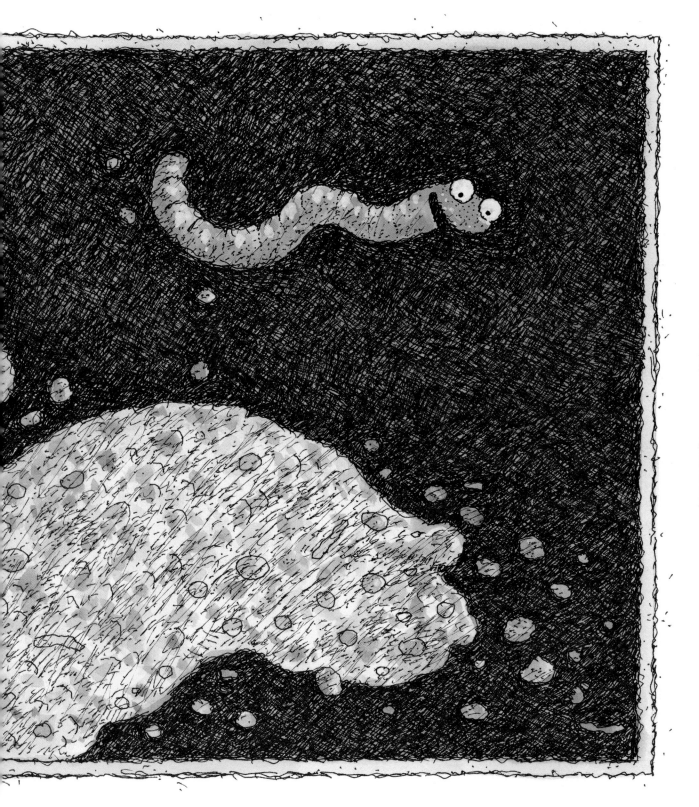

I don't know why she swallowed the worm,
but she started to squirm!

There was an old lady who swallowed a bee.
It happened quickly
when she swallowed the bee.

She swallowed the bee to rest on the flower.
She swallowed the flower to plant in the dirt.
She swallowed the dirt so the worm could wiggle.

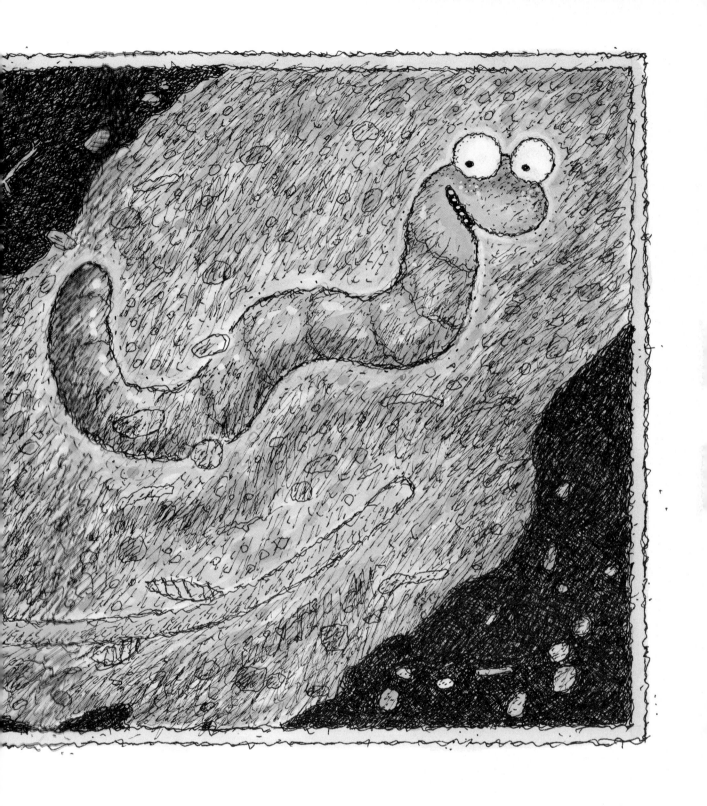

I don't know why she swallowed the worm,
but she started to squirm!

There was an old lady who swallowed a bird.
Oh, how absurd! To swallow a bird!

She swallowed the bird to fly with the bee.

She swallowed the bee to rest on the flower.
She swallowed the flower to plant in the dirt.
She swallowed the dirt so the worm could wiggle.

I don't know why she swallowed the worm,
but she started to squirm!

There was an old lady who swallowed a tree.
She was on a spree when she swallowed that tree.

She swallowed the tree so the bird would not flee.

She swallowed the bird to fly with the bee.

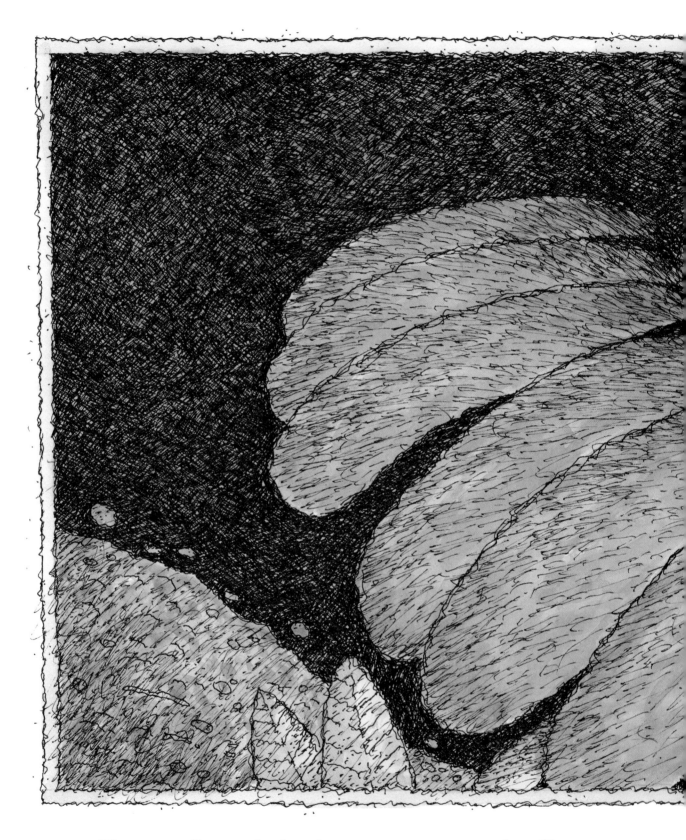

She swallowed the bee to rest on the flower.

She swallowed the flower to plant in the dirt.

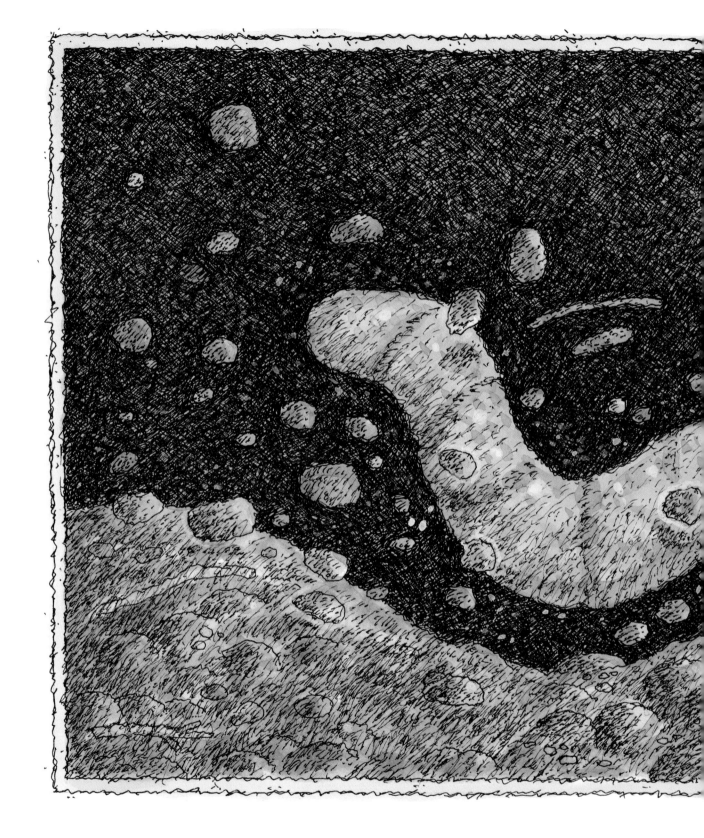

She swallowed the dirt so the worm could wiggle.

I don't know why she swallowed the worm,
but she started to squirm!

There was an old lady who swallowed a quilt.
She felt no guilt as she swallowed that quilt.

Then she hopped
on her bike
and shouted,
"Hooray!"

She just could not wait to celebrate Earth Day!